Series 522

MOSES
Prince and Shepherd

Told by LUCY DIAMOND
Illustrated by KENNETH INNS

Publishers: Ladybird Books Ltd . Loughborough
© Ladybird Books Ltd (formerly Wills & Hepworth Ltd) 1955
Printed in England

MOSES, PRINCE AND SHEPHERD

Long ago, in the days when Egypt was a great and powerful nation, a new king or Pharaoh came to the throne. This Pharaoh was proud of his wonderful country with its mighty buildings, its pyramids and temples, its strong armies, and its ships which sailed far across the seas.

But one thing did not please him. In a corner of his realm—the Land of Goshen—strangers were living. They were Hebrew shepherd folk, of the family of Joseph, the great Governor who had saved the Egyptians from death by famine.

Joseph's people had come to Egypt from Canaan at the invitation of the Pharaoh of that day, who had given them the Land of Goshen to live in. There they settled and lived in peace and safety.

4

0 7214 0153 8

Nearly three hundred years had gone by since Joseph died, and the Children of Israel, as his tribe were called, had prospered and increased. They worshipped the one true God, the Lord Jehovah, and never bowed down to the many heathen gods of the Egyptians.

Now this new Pharaoh cared nothing about Joseph, the Hebrew slave, whose wisdom and faith, when he became Governor, had saved the people from starvation. He hated and feared the Children of Israel.

" Look," he said, " they are as many in number as the sands of the sea! They are strong, and perhaps one day they will rise against us and drive us out of our own land." Pharaoh was really worried.

" We must do something about these people," he said.

The Children of Israel were ordered to leave their shepherding and do other work. Pharaoh made them into slaves, to toil all day in the hot sand under a scorching sun. He started building two enormous stone cities and all the heavy work was done by these Hebrew slaves. They had to make bricks and cut and haul huge blocks of stone during the hottest hours of the day. If they fainted or lagged behind in their work, there were taskmasters with cruel whips to drive them on. Many died under the scorching heat and the terrible whips, but, in spite of everything, there seemed to be more and more of these people whom Pharaoh hated.

He became furiously angry.

" I will destroy them in the end," he vowed.

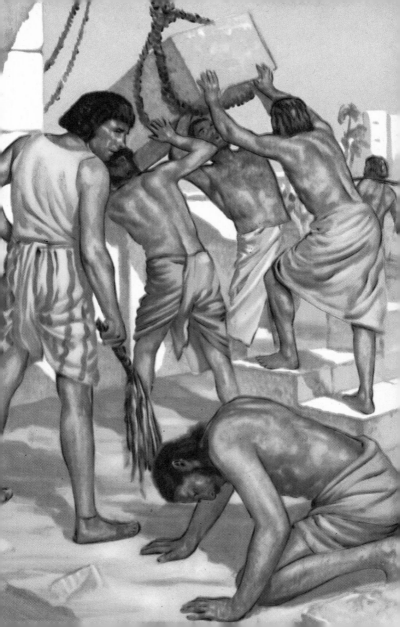

He gave orders to his soldiers: " Every baby boy that is born among the Children of Israel you must throw into the river. Let only the baby girls live."

Thus Pharaoh hoped to make certain that no baby boys were allowed to grow up into men who might fight against him. There was mourning in the Land of Goshen when Pharaoh's orders were obeyed. Many baby boys were thrown into Egypt's great river, the Nile.

Among the Hebrews was a faithful servant of the Lord Jehovah named Amram. His wife's name was Jochabed. They had two children—Miriam, and a little boy named Aaron. Then, just after the law was made, a baby boy was born. He was a lovely child, and his parents felt they must try to save him.

They told no one of his birth, and warned their two children not to speak of their baby brother.

For three months they managed to keep him safely hidden. Then they became afraid. The child was growing older, and any day someone might hear him crying and tell the soldiers. What could they do?

Amram and Jochabed prayed to the Lord Jehovah to help and guide them. Then Jochabed went down to the river Nile and gathered an armful of bulrushes—the strong papyrus reeds which grew thickly by its banks. Quickly she hurried home, and working secretly, she wove the reeds into a basket-work cradle—a little ark. She covered the outside with mud and pitch to keep out the water, and then put in a soft lining.

When her work was finished, Jochabed dressed her baby and laid him in the strange cradle. She covered him with his little quilt, and tucked him in to keep him safe and warm. Then she peeped out from the house to make sure that no one was about. All was quiet, so the anxious mother picked up the little ark and stole down to the river.

There she parted the thick reeds and laid the ark, which cradled her precious baby, on the water among them.

But Jochabed was still anxious, so she went home and called her daughter Miriam. Telling her where the ark was hidden, she said: " Go and stand a little way off and see what happens."

Miriam hid herself among the reeds, and watched and waited.

That day Pharaoh's daughter came down to bathe in the Nile. Her ladies were with her, laughing and talking as they walked along the river bank. All at once the Princess caught sight of something among the reeds.

" Look! " she cried, " what is that strange thing over there! "

One of her ladies went down to the water's edge and, parting the tall bulrushes, saw the little ark. She lifted it from the water and brought it to her mistress.

Pharaoh's daughter drew aside the soft covering, and there was a lovely babe, flushed and rosy with sleep.

But as she looked at him, the child woke up! When he saw the strange faces around him, he began to cry.

" Poor little mite! " said the Princess, and her face grew tender and pitiful.

" This is one of the Hebrew children," she said. " Some poor mother has hidden him here. But what a beautiful babe! We cannot let him be thrown into the river! "

She took the child into her arms, and he stopped crying.

" I must have him for my own," the Princess declared.

Now Miriam had been standing at a distance, hidden by a clump of tall rushes. She watched what happened, and when she saw Pharaoh's daughter take her baby brother so tenderly into her arms, she no longer felt afraid. She ventured from her hiding place, and as she drew nearer she heard what the Princess said.

Quickly Miriam slipped through the group of ladies, and stood before the gracious Princess who looked so sweet and kind.

" May I call you a nurse from among the Hebrew women? " she asked eagerly.

Pharaoh's daughter looked at the girl so anxiously awaiting her answer.

" Yes," she said thoughtfully. " Go and find me a nurse."

Joyfully Miriam hurried home, and in a few minutes Jochabed was running in breathless haste towards the river! There was the beautiful princess with the tiny child in her arms.

Eagerly the mother held out her own empty arms to take her baby into them.

Pharaoh's daughter looked into Jochabed's shining, happy eyes! Did she guess the truth as she said : " Take this child and nurse him for me, and I will pay you wages. When he is older bring him to me. He shall be my son. I shall call him Moses, because he was drawn from the water."

So Amram and Jochabed got back their baby and there was no need to be afraid. The soldiers would not dare to hurt the child whom Pharaoh's daughter had adopted. They gave thanks to the Lord Jehovah for the wonderful way in which their baby had been saved.

As the days and months passed, and Moses grew into a little boy, happy, strong and beautiful, they must have felt that God was watching over him in a special way. Perhaps one day he would be called upon to do some great work for the Lord Jehovah.

Within that happy home they taught him the faith of the Children of Israel. He learned to worship the Lord Jehovah—the God of Abraham, and Isaac, and Jacob —whose love was always around him.

But Pharaoh's daughter had not forgotten the child she had saved. When Moses was old enough, he was taken to her house to live there as her own son.

So this child of Hebrew parents became a Prince of Egypt. He lived in a palace with rich and beautiful things around him. Egypt was a thriving country, and Pharaoh's ships sailed far and near, bringing silks and ivories, gold and other precious treasures to make the palaces and temples colourful and magnificent.

The Egyptians were a very learned race. There were wise and clever men to teach Moses, and he learned to read and write in the strange " picture " writing which, even to-day, we may find inscribed or painted on ancient monuments or huge stones.

They taught him the mysteries of their strange religion. In their mighty temples he saw the Egyptian priests offer sacrifice and worship.

But the love and reverence for the Lord Jehovah which, in his first home, had been implanted in a child's heart still remained. This Hebrew boy was now living as a Prince in the palace of an Egyptian Princess, and being trained in the wisdom and knowledge of a highly civilised people. This training was specially fitting him for a great work which one day he would be called upon to do.

For God was watching over His people, and even as their miserable slavery seemed hopeless, the one who was to be their deliverer had been saved from death by the daughter of the very king who tortured and oppressed them.

Years passed, and Moses had grown into a strong, stalwart youth—every inch a Prince, with his rich clothing, his handsome, clean-shaven face, and his hair dressed like an Egyptian nobleman.

Yet in his heart he was still a Hebrew. He knew that the rough, bearded slaves toiling in the scorching sun were his own people. Their misery worried him and he wished he could help them.

One day, he saw a taskmaster with a cruel whip mercilessly beating a fainting Hebrew slave. Moses was so angry that he wrenched the whip from the man, struck him with it, and killed him.

When he realised what he had done, Moses anxiously looked around. There was no one about but the unconscious slave, so he hurriedly buried the Egyptian's body in the sand.

The next day Moses went out, and as he walked along he saw two Hebrews fighting. He was sorry to see that, so he hurried to try to part them.

"Oh, sirs," he said, "you are brothers. Why are you fighting each other like this?"

One of the men turned furiously upon the young Prince.

"How dare you try to interfere with us," he shouted. "Who made you a judge and a ruler over us? Do you mean to kill us, even as you killed the Egyptian yesterday?"

Then Moses knew that what he had done was known. He was afraid! He knew that when the thing came to Pharaoh's ears, he would have him killed. When he got back to the palace he found that the story was being whispered everywhere.

That night Moses secretly left the palace and fled for his life. He dared not leave Egypt by the main traveller's road. That way was guarded and he would soon have been captured.

He went by a lonely track which led south between the mountains and the Red Sea. Day and night he toiled on, hardly daring to rest until he came round by the mountains of Sinai into the Land of Midian.

Now he was beyond the country ruled by Pharaoh and, that terrible journey over, at last he could safely rest.

Not far away a few palm trees showed that there was a well. Moses was tired and thirsty, and the trees would give welcome shelter from the scorching heat.

So he made his way towards them and sat down by the well.

Jethro, the priest of Midian, had seven daughters, and they looked after their father's sheep. As Moses was sitting by the well they came there with their flocks. They drew water from the well and filled the troughs for the sheep to drink.

Just as they had made everything ready, some shepherds came and tried to drive the girls away. To save themselves trouble they meant to use the water in the troughs for their own sheep.

Then Moses stood up and made those selfish shepherds stand back. He helped the girls, and drew more water for them until all their flocks were satisfied and they could lead them home.

Only then would he let the other shepherds come near, and that day those unkind men had to draw water for themselves.

When Jethro's daughters got home their father was surprised. He knew how often rough shepherds had driven the girls from the well and made them wait until last to water their sheep.

" How is it that you are back so soon to-day? " he asked.

" A stranger who looked like an Egyptian prince was by the well," they answered. " He made the shepherds stand back, and then helped us draw water."

" Where is he? " Jethro asked his daughters. " Surely you did not leave the man by the well ! Go at once and bring him here. We must offer him food and shelter."

So Moses was brought to the house of the priest of Midian. Jethro liked this young man who had helped his daughters, and invited Moses to stay with them.

From that day Moses lived in Jethro's house. The priest of Midian was a wise, kindly man, and the two became firm friends.

Moses married Zipporah, one of Jethro's daughters, and then he looked after his father-in-law's flocks.

Now the young man who had lived as a prince and had been trained in all the learning of the Egyptians, was content to live as a shepherd, even as for ages his own people the Hebrews had done.

Perhaps sometimes as he watched his sheep Moses thought of those Children of Israel and their sufferings. In his anger he had tried to help them—but it seemed that he had utterly failed.

The Pharaoh who had sought to kill him was now dead, but another Pharaoh was treating the Hebrew slaves even more cruelly.

Years passed, and still Moses lived as a shepherd.

One day he led the sheep into the wilderness, and came to Horeb, the Mount of God. Suddenly he saw a bush aflame with fire !

Not an unusual sight in that hot country. The strange thing was that, though it burned furiously, the bush was not destroyed !

" That is queer," Moses thought, as he turned aside to look.

But a Voice called from the bush, " Moses ! Moses !"

Moses knew at once that this was the Voice of God. " Here I am," he answered.

" Do not come nearer," the Voice commanded. " Put your shoes from off your feet, for the place on which you stand is holy ground."

So Moses took off his shoes, as Eastern people always do, to show reverence when they go into a temple.

Once more the Voice spoke from the bush. "I am the God of your fathers—Abraham, Isaac, and Jacob."

Moses hid his face. He was afraid to look upon God.

"Moses, I have work for you to do. I have seen the sorrows of my people Israel. I will save them, and bring them from Egypt into the Land of Canaan—the land I promised to Abraham. Now I am sending you to Pharaoh. You shall lead my people out of Egypt !"

Moses was startled and afraid !

Humbly he answered, " Who am I, that I should go to Pharaoh and lead these people from his land ? "

" You must go," the Lord Jehovah answered. " I will surely be with you, and when you bring Israel from Egypt you shall all worship me upon this mountain."

" When you get to Egypt, go to Pharaoh and ask him to let you go three days' journey into the wilderness to sacrifice to the Lord your God. He will not let you go at first, but in the end he will. I will smite Egypt with many terrible things."

" But suppose the people do not believe me," Moses pleaded.

" What is that in your hand ?" the Voice replied.

" A rod," said Moses.

" Cast it on the ground."

Moses did so, and it became a serpent from which he fled in terror.

" Put out your hand and take it by the tail." Moses obeyed, and it became once more a rod in his hand.

" That is one sign," the Lord said, " and I will show you many others to make them believe."

But Moses still hesitated !

" Oh, my Lord," he said, " I am slow of speech ! How can I venture to talk to the Children of Israel ? "

Then the Lord Jehovah was angry.

" I will teach you what you shall say," He said, "but your brother Aaron can speak well. He shall go with you. You must be the Leader, and tell him what to do, and he shall speak for you. Now go back to Egypt. The men are dead who wanted to kill you. But take the rod of God in your hand."

Moses hurried home and found Jethro.

" Will you let me go back to Egypt," he asked. " I want to see if my people are still alive."

The wise old priest saw that something strange had happened, but he asked no questions.

" Go in peace," he said.

Moses made ready for a long journey. Jethro gave him asses for Zipporah and her children to ride, and to carry food and baggage. They said a loving farewell, and Jethro sadly watched the little caravan out of sight.

And far away in Egypt, a message had come to Aaron the Levite. The Lord Jehovah spoke to him.

" Go out into the wilderness to meet Moses your brother. He is coming back to Egypt."

Aaron was surprised, but at once he prepared for the journey, and his sister Miriam helped him. How excited they must have felt at the thought of seeing Moses again ! Aaron took the road by the Red Sea, so the two brothers were journeying towards each other. They met in Horeb, the Mount of God.

How eagerly Aaron ran to his long-lost brother and kissed him ! Then, when he had greeted Zipporah and the children, the two sat down to talk.

Moses told Aaron what had happened, and of the mighty task which lay before them. He spoke with quiet confidence. He knew that they went in the power of the Lord Jehovah, and in that strength, and not at the urge of his own quick temper, would Israel be saved !

Then Aaron realised for what Divine purpose a little child had been saved from the river long years before.

Steadfastly the brothers set their faces towards Egypt to obey the Lord's command. But how Moses, the faithful servant of Jehovah, became the great Leader of a great people, and triumphantly shepherded them from Egypt, is another story.

Series 522